All I Need

Spirits of Laken 1

By
Eden Ashe

Copyright © 2016 by Eden Ashe
ISBN: 978-1-68361-010-6
Cover art by Mina Carter

Published by Decadent Publishing Company, LLC
Look for us online at:
www.decadentpublishing.com

Praise for *All I Need*

Ashe has the same knack to make her characters leap off the page and land straight into your heart ~ Amazon Reviewer

Passion sizzled on every page, and the ever-present sexual tension between Jilly and Luke is a boiling tea kettle of emotion right from the start ~ Amazon Reviewer

This is a SEARING HOT read and hopefully when Ashe is done writing this hero, she can just send him direct to me! Worst part of the book was that it had to end. This book needs to come with a "WARNING: BOOK HANGOVER AHEAD" label ~ Amazon Reviewer

~A Note from the Author~

Dear Reader,

Jilly and Luke were the first couple in my head. I'd never wanted to be a writer, or even thought I'd be able to do it if I did. But after years of devouring romance novels, I woke up one morning to find a tiny, spunky, slightly-damaged Jilly already madly in love with Luke. He was the small-town good boy, and after one meeting with Jilly, he knew she was meant to be his.

The first draft of their story was 170,000 words. 600+ pages. It was like once I started writing—and writing them—they didn't want me to ever quit. But finally, I was able to get them to their much deserved happy ending.

After that, they sat on my hard drive through five new computers, patiently waiting while I worked on other couples. Then, out of the blue, Luke spoke up. All he said was "Now." I thought about pretending I didn't know what he was talking about, but I figured these two had waited long enough. Only when I started on them, they decided they'd gotten the majority of their issues worked out in their first draft all those years ago, so this time, they wanted to have fun.

I love this story. I love these characters. They're everything I love to write, and they love each other *so much.*

I hope you enjoy reading them as much as I enjoyed writing them. Feel free to contact me at edenashe@gmail.com.

Dedication

To Mary, thank you for being you. Loves ya, my friend.

Chapter One

The high-pitched squeal blasted her eardrums the second Jilly opened her car door. Bracing for the coming impact, she'd barely slid out from behind the wheel when the tall, willowy body of her best friend hit her. Losing her balance, Jilly landed on her butt in the dirt, Megan Bannon wrapped around her, a grin lighting up her flawless, beautiful face.

"You're here!" Megan squealed again. She cupped Jilly's face in her hands and gave her a huge, smacking kiss on the mouth. "I was starting to think you'd changed your mind about coming."

Jilly grimaced. "And risk my grandmother coming back to haunt me? No thank you." She tried to shove her off, but it got her nowhere. Megan had six inches on her. Instead, Jilly dug her finger into the woman's rib cage, her one ticklish spot. "Would you get off me,

1

you oaf?"

Snickering, Megan leapt to her feet with the casual grace of a born dancer and held out her hand to help her up. "I can't believe you're finally home for good." She hugged her once more before she moved to the back of Jilly's car, popped the trunk, and peered inside. Frowning, she asked, "That's it?"

Jilly shrugged and grabbed the first box. "I have to get the house sorted and figure out what to do with all of Nana's stuff. She's always been borderline hoarder, and Luke said it only got worse the last couple of years. I didn't want to bring more clutter into it." Because it still hurt to think about her grandmother, even five months after her death, Jilly blew out a breath. "Is he here?"

Megan snagged a box then lifted a perfect blonde brow. "Who? My pain-in-the-ass brother? Not yet." She muttered something Jilly couldn't hear before bumping her hip. "You're not going to kill him, are you?"

Because she'd had to leave right after her grandmother's funeral to get back to her job, she hadn't been able to stay for the will reading. Which meant she still had no clue why Nana had left half of Jilly's ancestral home to her best friend's big brother.

The lawyer had only said her Nana's will had been specific—if Jilly didn't have a husband by the time Nana died, half of the entire estate went to her. The other half went to Luke.

Shaking her head, she started up the broken stone path to the home she'd grown up in, half expecting to see her grandmother tending to her prize roses in one of the dozen sprawling gardens. Ignoring the pain in her chest at the realization that Nana really was gone, she focused on the house in front of her.

Crisp, bright-white, half-farmhouse and half-Victorian, with a single spire piercing the sky from the middle and no two windows or doors the same, St. James Manor had sprawled over Laken, South Carolina for four generations.

"Hey." Megan stopped walking so abruptly, Jilly almost ran into her. Her friend scowled at her over her shoulder. "You know it worries me when you go quiet like this. Tell me you're not planning anything...stupid."

More amused than offended, Jilly scooted around her and continued toward the house. "Just because I don't understand why your brother inherited half of my family's house, doesn't mean I'm going to murder him in his sleep, Megs."

"Ha." She let out an unladylike snort. "I'd believe that more if you two weren't mortal enemies."

Juggling the box in one arm, she searched her pocket for her keys. "I don't hate him, and he's not my enemy."

"Please." Megan rolled her eyes. "You two have never been able to stay in a room together."

Jilly stopped halfway up the front porch steps, something tightening in her gut. Shifting the box into the crook of one arm, she grabbed Meg's wrist until their eyes locked. "Maybe once, but it's kind of hard to hate the person who saved your life. Twice. Literally."

Pure, unadulterated rage flashed in the depths of Megan's glass-green eyes at the remembrance of what had triggered her brother's temper. "Luke was too nice. That asshole deserved to die."

As always, love swamped Jilly at her immediate, wholehearted jump to over-protective best friend. Going on tiptoe, she kissed her cheek then drew in a long, slow breath and squared off with the large, hand-carved front door. "All right, are you ready?"

Megan bobbed her head. "When you are."

With the box still tucked under one arm, Jilly grasped the handle. Before she could turn the knob, her fingers slipped off. She tried again.

Megan's head canted when, after the third try, Jilly had only managed to wrap her hand around the knob. "What the hell? Is it greased?"

Shaking her head, Jilly set the box on the porch then swiped her palms across the backof her jeans. Her hands weren't sweaty, and the knob didn't feel different—the handle was normal. But no matter what she did, she couldn't hold onto it.

"Let me try." Megan dumped her box in Jilly's arms then made a production of pretending to crack her knuckles before she gripped the knob without luck. They stared at each other. "Okay, I'm calling it. That's officially weird."

Jilly shook her head again and handed the box back to her, half-positive they were missing something. Who couldn't open a door? "Stay here. I'll go try the back door."

✳✳✳

As bad days went, Luke Bannon figured this one had to be in the fucking hall of fame.

Five months. For five goddamned months, he and his lawyers had been searching for a way out.

Something, some small loophole that would get him out of ownership of a white elephant he had no desire to co-own, let alone deal with.

He had enough shit going on in his life without worrying about some damn money pit monstrosity, or the woman who came along with it. But despite everything, despite all the money he'd paid them to find a way out, his lawyers had informed him the damn will was ironclad.

To unload the beast, he'd have to sell it, and he didn't have to imagine what Jilly's reaction to that would be: Over her dead body.

Tossing his toolbox into the passenger seat of his ancient truck, he climbed behind the wheel and told himself to man-up and face the facts—he was good and royally fucked.

Pushing a palm through the hair he'd forgotten to get trimmed—again—he thought there had to be away to appeal to her common sense. Despite her emotional attachment to the place, Jilly had to see that, for one, it was too goddamn big for her. And, two, the place needed so much work, even if he started that day, it would take him ten years to renovate and update everything.

Which exhausted him just thinking about it.

6

But, being honest, it wasn't her reaction that worried him. He knew her, how she'd react, and he wouldn't blame her for any of it. St. James Manor belonged to her family, the last thing she had left of her parents and her grandparents, and she belonged there.

So, no. He didn't expect any surprises there. It was himself he worried about. He could fight through the lawyers until the end of time, but when he came face-to-face with her, he'd damn well give her the moon if she asked for it.

And since the terms of the will were clear-cut and ironclad, Luke had two choices—convince her to sell her ancestral home or move in with her.

The lawyers had given him clear indication before he'd left their office; he had one week to convince her to sell. That was it.

He may as well pack his fucking bags and move in.

Spotting her car when he took the turn up into the long, winding drive, he pulled in behind it, set his jaw, and yanked the last box out of her open trunk before starting up the path.

His steps faltered at the sight that greeted him. Megan sat on the steps of the huge wraparound porch, giving directions to Jilly, who crouched on her hands and knees—ass facing him—in the bushes, trying to.... nothing came to mind.

"What the hell are you doing?"

All movement stopped with a squeak, and a muffled *oh shit* emanated from the shrubbery before she backed out. Shooting to her feet, she was all grace and dignity as she clasped her hands in front of her and offered him a cheerful smile.

"Hi."

Lust, raw, painful, and grinding, slammed into him with so much force, he almost staggered under it. And, quick on the heels of the lust, came the blinding need. To touch her. Feel her. Wrap her in his arms and never fucking let her go.

Instead, he glared at her, torn between self-preservation and self-loathing for the light that dimmed in her sky-blue eyes. "What are you doing?"

Small and curvy, with dark-red hair, a perfect Cupid's-bow mouth, and freckles, she was the perfect mix of adorably cute and heart-stoppingly beautiful. The banked, tightly controlled fire in her eyes never failed to gut him. If he were less of a man, and if she weren't his little sister's best friend, he'd have devoted his life to tempting that fire until it burned them both alive.

8

An upturned chin was her only outward sign of emotion. "There is something wrong with the doors. I was trying to break in through the basement window."

He frowned. "What are you talking about?" Without waiting for an answer, he moved past her and took the porch steps two at a time. The two women whispered to each other behind him, but he ignored them and grasped the knob. It turned easily, the door swinging open as if it had been waiting for him.

"What?" Jilly and Megan asked in stunned unison.

His sister poked him in the back. "How did you do that?"

Dropping the box he held onto the nearest decorative table, he propped his shoulder against the wall and narrowed his eyes. "Are you two drinking already?"

With one final glare at him, Jilly pulled the door shut then immediately opened it again. "How...?" She raked a hand through her shoulder-length hair and looked at Megan. "Are we cracking up?"

"Yes," he said at the same moment his sister said, "No."

They continued taking turns closing the door and

opening it again. Desperation already ground low in his gut, and watching her wasn't helping.

The coming week wasn't just going to be the hardest of his life. It would never fucking end.

Chapter Two

oly crap, Luke Bannon is hot.

At six foot three, and nothing but thick, solid muscle, he should have been a bull in a china shop in Jilly's grandmother's house, with all its delicate furniture and piles and piles of glass knickknacks. But, despite his ginormous size, he strode through the clutter to put her boxes down with confidence and ease, perfectly at home.

Light-brown, slightly wavy hair peeked out from underneath the same Cubs hat he'd worn since they were kids, shielding mismatched eyes. One green, one brown. A new tattoo snaked down his left arm, and, if she had to guess, probably something dark and monstrous. A genuine, hard-working good guy, he'd been into horror books and movies since childhood.

A finger dug into her rib cage. "Jills, geez. Are you

listening to me? I have to go."

Dragging her gaze away from Luke, she blinked up at Megan. "What?"

Meg bent and laid the back of her hand on Jilly's brow. "What's wrong with you? Are you feeling all right?"

Out of the corner of her eye, Jilly saw Luke's head snap up, and he swung around to stare at her. Embarrassed, she swatted the hand away. "I'm fine." She ducked away from her to move farther into the living room. Big mistake.

The lingering scent of her grandmother's perfume hit her and knocked her off balance. Tears burned her eyes as she stood, unable to move as years of memories washed over her.

"Oh, honey." Megan wrapped her arms around her from behind, rested her chin on her shoulder, and squeezed. "It's okay."

Luke cleared his throat. "I'll leave you alone." He tugged the brim of his cap lower over his eyes.

Jilly swiped the tears away and shook her head then rested it against Megan's. "I'm all right; it just took me a minute." Then, feeling steadier, she blew out a breath and glanced at Luke. "Didn't you bring anything?"

Irritation flashed over his face. "It's in my truck." After scooting a waist-high pile of magazines off the stairs and onto the floor, he sat on the vacated spot. He braced his arms on his thighs and rolled his neck. "So, we're really doing this?"

Megan shot a look-half surprise, half confusion between them before backing toward the door. "I think that's my cue. Jilly, I love you, and I'll call you tomorrow. Luke, Mom wants you to call her."

And then Meg bailed, leaving Jilly alone with her brother. Shoving her hands into the back pockets of her jeans, she tried to look anywhere except at the man lounging on her stairs. While Jilly and Luke had known each other all of their lives, the last time she'd seen him, she'd been in the hospital with several broken bones, courtesy of her ex-boyfriend.

Luke had stayed with her until the doctors had released her, growling and intimidating the entire staff until he'd been sure they'd be nice to her. But, once her grandmother had arrived to take care of her, he'd disappeared.

That had been five years earlier.

As if his mind had traveled to the same place hers had, he asked, "Megan said everything healed properly after...."

She curled her lip in disgust. "I call him Dickhead Asshat."

"Fitting. I like it." His mismatched gaze scanned the large room again before settling on her. "My lawyer said the terms are clear; we have one week to make a decision."

Their lawyers had been in constant contact, and wanted Luke to sell the house. While she didn't blame him, it wasn't his ancestral home. It was hers. And even if she could afford to buy him out—she couldn't—they had a non-negotiable contract. Either they agreed to sell it, or they had to live in it together.

Seeing as he was the ultimate bachelor and she had dreams of turning St. James Manor into a boutique gift store, complete with artwork by local painters, their living together wouldn't work.

But she'd be damned if she gave into the alternative and sold her family's home.

It didn't help that he'd always treated her like one of his little sisters. No matter that Jilly and Megan were both twenty five, he still insisted he knew what was best for both of them.

Not sure what to do, she wandered around the space and tried to figure out where to start.

"You could hire someone to come and box it all up,

then put it in storage until you're ready to deal with it," Luke said, his voice gentler than he'd ever directed at her. His voice rough-edged, it sounded as though he had to force every word spoken to her out against his will.

Moving over, she sat on the step below him, so close to him her shoulder bumped his thigh. Unprepared for the jolt of sheer, unrestrained need that shocked her down to her toes, she gasped.

"I might." She turned and braced her back against the wall, giving her a better angle to study his beautifully rugged face. "Eventually. Right now, it kind of feels like it should be my responsibility. You know?"

Luke swallowed hard. He clenched his hands into fists, and still, the need to grab her and devour her was so fierce, he trembled with it.

Get a grip, Bannon. They were talking about her newly dead grandmother's belongings. Not exactly the time to be fantasizing about one thousand different ways he could unleash Jilly's fiery side in bed.

When the lecture did no good, his body not cooperating with his decision to keep her at a distance, since he hadn't been this close to her in five years—five long, goddamned years—he sprang to his feet and headed for the door where she'd left the rest of her boxes. But when he reached it, it wouldn't open.

"What the hell?"

She let out a loud *ha!* "I'm not cracking up! I told you the door was screwy."

He glared over his shoulder in time to see her jump to her feet and give a quick little hip boogie. *Christ.* How had he forgotten how fucking cute her happy dances were?

"Do you mind?" Deliberately using his best stern voice, the one that had the men on his crew shaping right the hell up, had no effect on her. She only grinned and did it again. "This could be a problem, Jilly."

With a roll of her eyes, she stopped dancing and plopped her hands on her luscious hips. "There are other exits, Luke." She said his name in the same tone he'd said hers, half in frustration, half in humor as she headed toward the kitchen at the back of the house. "It's not like we're locked in here." He followed her to the back door and not simply to watch her perfect ass in skin-tight jeans. Her back stiffened with her hand on the doorknob and gave it a fruitless twist. "Okay, I'm willing to admit this may be a problem."

Christ alive, she smelled good. Barely managing to stop before burying his face in her hair and getting a better sniff of her, he stood behind her and wrapped one arm around her slender waist. With an indrawn breath, he reached over her shoulder to try the handle.

His hand slid right off. He scowled because he'd replaced the door—hinges, frames, hardware, all of it— only a few months earlier.

After trying one more time, he let her nudge his arm out of the way to give it another shot. When it didn't work, she scooted around him and over to the kitchen window.

Despite his growing concern, he had to chuckle when she opened the bottom cabinet door, stepped into it, and used the leverage to hoist herself up onto the counter. Propping a shoulder against the door, he crossed his arms and grinned. "You know, I could have gotten that for you."

With a glare in her pretty eyes, she repeated his words in a mock-angry, sarcastic voice then said, "Not funny, Bannon. I'm not that short."

"Sure. Keep telling yourself that, St. James." Lifting an eyebrow, he made a show of bending sideways to get a better look at what she was doing. "Don't forget to unlock it."

She gave what could only be described as a growl. A feminine, wholly cute growl, and his eye twitched. Jilly had always been so much goddamn fun to tease.

After pointing a finger at him in warning, she returned her attention to the window and he had to admit, he could stand there all day watching her move and stretch while trying to get that damn window open.

Finally, he stepped forward and grabbed her off the counter. Though he ignored her indignant squeak, the shock of her in his arms sent his lust into overdrive.

Mine.

He'd known it for years. Since the night he'd found her broken and terrified, courtesy of the bastard she'd been dating. The rage that had flooded through his system had been beyond anything he'd ever experienced—beyond what he'd always thought was leftover emotion because of her attachment to his sisters. As if someone had picked his world up, flipped it upside down, spun it a few hundred times, then sat him back in the middle of it. He'd had no idea what to do with the emotion, except he had to take care of her then figure it out later.

While Megan had kept him updated on Jilly's life, boyfriends and all, he'd cut off all contact with her. At first, it had been because he'd disappeared off the map to drag the bastard out of the hole he'd hidden in to escape charges. Then, after Luke had put the asshole in the hospital, the last thing Jilly'd needed was a hovering beast of a male who couldn't keep his feelings for her in check.

After that, she'd moved on. Finished college, found a new life on the opposite side of the country, and forgotten about her best friend's brother. Because she'd never see him as anything else.

And five years had passed.

"Luke?" The whisper-soft voice dragged him out of his head, and he lowered his gaze to hers. She watched him out of wide eyes, confusion flickering in their depths. "Are you going to put me down?"

"In a minute." *Fuck no*. "Let me try the window first."

"I don't think you need me in your arms to do that." She poked his shoulder, and tried to wiggle out of his arms. In an instant his cock became diamond-

19

hard and he had to drop her. The second her feet touched the floor, he was on the far side of the room, bent over at the waist and trying to catch his breath.

What the hell is happening to me?

Chapter Three

Luke didn't know what the hell was wrong with him, but he didn't like it. Something vicious burned in his chest, lighting his heart on fire, his jeans were ten sizes too small against his cock, and lust raged through him. Like a goddamned fifteen year old who'd somehow managed to come face-to-face with the naked woman of his dreams. Only Jilly wasn't naked, and he had no intention of letting their relationship ever hit that point. Besides, he hadn't exactly been a monk the last few years. And since she'd never know how he felt about her, he wouldn't feel guilty over it, either.

Even if it seemed wrong.

A blast of air hit him, so cold his bones ached.

Soft footsteps sounded behind him, before Jilly bent sideways and stuck her face underneath his. That quickly, the cold spot disappeared. The concern in her blue eyes staggered him and he had to clench his fists again to keep from reaching for her.

She tipped the brim of his cap up, out of his eyes, to study them better. "Luke? What's wrong?"

"Nothing." He grunted at her, and forced himself to straighten. When she followed him, he glared at her. "Forget it. We need to check the rest of the windows in this place."

For a moment, when she continued to stare, her gaze searching his face, he worried she'd push the issue. The last thing he wanted was to be a dick to her, but they were both better off if she didn't how far gone he was over her.

Putting as much space between them as he could in the house would be the best plan he'd had in...ever. But he'd only made it halfway across the kitchen before her slender fingers wrapped around his wrist, and she tried to tug him to a stop. "Hey."

Christ. She had to stop touching him. Yanking his arm away, he backed up, not giving a shit he looked like a cowardly ass. He was and he had no problem admitting it.

"Look, sweetheart." Not sure what to do with himself, he shoved his fists into the pockets of his jeans. "We're not friends, all right? You're my little sister's best friend, and I'm only here to convince you to sell this place. That's it."

Hurt flickered over her face, and she took a step away from him. "Got it." She headed for the stairs. "I'll check the top floor windows."

He didn't give in to the need to go after her. Every cell in his body wanted to chase her down, apologize for being a huge dick, and lay it all out for her.

Instead, he checked the first floor doors again, then moved down to the cellar. Despite the warm day, the cellar was frigid. The temperature continued to drop to a violent, dangerous level the deeper he went. He gritted his teeth against the chill, checked the windows, and sighed in relief when he escaped to the second floor.

When he still hadn't heard from her a half hour later, he took the stairs to the third floor three at a time. "Jilly?"

Christ, how could one place have so many rooms, alcoves and room-sized closets? And *stuff*? He couldn't even identify half the crap in the place, but he'd come to the conclusion Jilly's grandmother had owned enough blankets and pillows and towels to warm the North Pole.

"Jilly?" Worry churned in his gut. While he didn't

want to panic, they were locked in this place. And if something could lock them in, there was no telling what else it would be able to do. "If you're buried under linens or angel figurines, I need you to let me know."

Instead of an answer, he found the stairs to the attic. Thin and old, and hanging by chains instead of railings, they were unsafe as all hell, but he had no idea where else to look.

Praying to whatever god wanted to listen that the warped wood would hold his enormous weight, he squared his shoulders and started up them. By the time he got to the top, the urge to lecture her for risking herself without him being there to catch her if she fell burned a hole through his tongue.

"This is not funny, St. James." Ducking under the low ceiling beam, he squinted, trying to see through the dust filling the air.

Nearby, the distinct, terrifying sound of sniffling reached him right before he spotted her curled up in a dormer window seat, her knees to her chest.

Shit.

"Hey, don't cry." He walked, half-hunched, toward the far side of the cramped space. Damn sure he had to be the biggest asshole on the planet, he crouched beside her. "I didn't mean to be an ass, baby."

She rolled her eyes and swiped her palm across her cheeks. "I'm pretty sure we're locked in here."

He lowered next to her and pulled his knees up, resting his forearms against them. "Yeah. I came to the same conclusion." All doubts and lectures forgotten, he brushed a damp curl off her cheek. "I am sorry."

"I'm not crying because of you." One blue-tipped finger wiped at her tears again. "Well, not just because of you." She brushed at her tears again and looked down at him, putting her so close to him her beautiful face filled his vision. Her sweet scent, like wildflowers in the rain, would have knocked him on his ass if he wasn't already there. "It's being back here without her. I thought I'd prepared myself for the hurt."

He silently cursed. Damn it, he should have thought. Should have remembered how much she'd adored her grandmother, even if everyone else in town could barely tolerate the old bat.

Rising, he grabbed her hand and pulled her to her feet. "Come on. Let's go get you some water then figure out how to get out of this place."

***

Luke was acting...weird. Not just that he'd snapped at her for the first time in her life, though that had surprised her on more than one level. He'd always been a stable, cool-headed giant of a man. Even when he'd get frustrated with one of his sisters, usually after they'd disobeyed him and ended up hurt or in trouble, he'd still barely raised his voice.

But though he'd pulled her off the window seat, he didn't move. Simply stared at her with a shuttered look in his eyes that had her belly tingling and her thighs trembling.

She sucked in a breath when his gaze dropped to her mouth. She should run for her life, but her knees weakened at the sheer hunger in his face. Luke Bannon could eat her alive without breaking a sweat.

And *dear God,* she wanted him to.

Confused and unable to do anything about the way her nipples puckered beneath the thin fabric of her T-shirt, she returned his gaze, afraid if she blinked, she'd break whatever spell caused him to look at her—her, for cripes sake—that way.

"Luke?" She kept her voice soft, her nerve endings

26

tingling as he ducked his head toward hers and angled his body closer, so if she took a deep enough breath, her breasts would brush against that solid wall of abs. "I...."

The words were forgotten as his hand came up to tangle in her hair. The callused pad of his thumb brushed over her cheek, her bottom lip, then dipped between her lips before he brought it to his mouth and swiped his tongue over the tip. "Jesus. I knew you'd be sweet."

"What?" She ignored the breathy tone of her voice. "You've thought about how I'd taste?"

"No. Yes. Goddamn it." In one quick, dizzying move, he had her pressed against the wall next to the window seat, his giant-sized body nearly covering her from head to foot. His mismatched eyes burned into hers, and she suddenly wanted more than anything in the world for him to make good on the dark, wicked promises in them.

"Just once, baby. Let me taste you one time, then I swear to God, I'll leave you alone. I'll sign the goddamn house over to you, whatever you want. Just...please. Kiss me."

She didn't know what knocked her off balance more—that he wanted to kiss her, or he wanted it enough to beg. And then one large hand wrapped around the back of her neck while the other grasped her hip and yanked her up against his straining cock.

Because denying him suddenly felt like cutting off one of her own limbs, she nodded and strained up on her toes to fasten her mouth to his.

Shock rippled through both of them. Jilly moaned as need—hot and fast and dangerous—tore through her, consuming her, while he let out a raw, starving sound and somehow managed to pull her closer. His hips ground into her, hitting that perfect spot between her legs, where she needed him most, over and over until his strong arm hooking around her waist became the only thing holding her up.

"Luke." Without her permission, her hands were under his shirt, her greedy fingers busy tracing over hard, bulging muscle. His magic mouth destroyed her defenses and ate her up at the same time, until she couldn't remember her own name. "Don't stop."

"Can't. Can't stop, baby." He hitched her up suddenly and changed the angle of the kiss, somehow taking them deeper. His tongue took, conquered, offered. Devoured. When she wrapped her legs around his waist, he shifted her so she fitted right where they both desperately needed him. Where she ached. Desperately.

Jilly had never been kissed with so much focus before. Like it wasn't about the possibility of sex, but *her* that he needed. Like he needed a taste of her, the feel of her, so much he couldn't get enough of her. And though her hands were busy exploring and touching, all of his concentration focused on her mouth.

She was boneless when he finally pulled back to let them both breathe. Her brain had short-circuited until the house and her grandmother were forgotten and the only thought in her brain centered on how to get him to do that again.

More importantly, how to get him to do more. All.

Megan would kill her for the thoughts, but Jilly couldn't remember why that mattered. Then the words tumbled out before she'd given her brain the okay to say them. "Can we do that again?"

Chapter Four

He'd lost his mind. It was that simple. And that fucked up. Because once he'd discovered what she tasted like, he would never stop craving her.

Worse, so goddamn much worse—she'd responded to him like she needed him, too. Like years of passion had been unlocked inside her, igniting her into something so fiery and greedy, he'd been terrified he'd be lost forever in the brilliance of her.

Her question rang in his head, tempting him and drowning out every ounce of common sense he'd ever possessed. His body trembled with the need to taste her again, to feel her perfect curves mold into his body and see how far she'd let him take them.

But even then, if he gave in to the need, he wouldn't be able to stop. There would be no holding himself in check, no remembering his rules or reasons for keeping his feelings to himself.

Denying her felt like slicing his own heart out of his chest. Pain tore through him, but he kept his gaze locked on hers. "No." Dropping his hands to his sides, he moved around her, heading toward the attic stairs. "We can't do this again."

"What?" The simple brush of her fingertips against his skin when she grabbed his wrist, nearly shattered his resolve. She darted in front of him, her eyes dark with lust and confusion. "Why not?"

He untangled his arm from her grip as gently as he could. "Because we're adults, Jilly. There are some things I'm not willing to risk."

She planted her feet and crossed her arms, daring him to go through her. "What does that mean?"

Sure if he didn't get out of the tiny space soon, he would lose the last thread of sanity he managed to hold onto, he grasped her by the upper arms and lifted her off her feet. Shifting slightly, he set her to the side to let the attic stairs down. He frowned, not recalling that he'd pulled them up after him.

"Luke?" She knelt next to him, her voice soft and confused. "What's wrong?"

The latch was stuck. Tipping his ball cap back for a better view in the limited light coming through the windows, he shifted and put his weight into opening it.

The latch snapped off in his hand. Below them, doors slammed shut.

"Oh, shit," Jilly breathed.

He sat back on his heels and scrubbed both hands over his face. "Yeah. Oh, shit." Pulling his cell phone out of his back pocket, he dialed his father from memory then tucked the phone between his shoulder and ear and got to his feet. When the phone did nothing but give him a *no-signal* beep, tendrils of worry spread through his gut. The house, up on a hill and surrounded by the ocean on three sides, had always been a technology black hole. He tried Megan's phone and, when he got the same response, he considered chucking his phone across the room.

Shoving it back in his pocket, he put his considerable weight into trying to kick the door hatch open.

"Hey." Jilly slipped her small hand into his. "You're going to hurt yourself."

He grunted and tried again. "We have no food. No way to call out, and who knows when anyone will come looking for us. A sore leg seems worth it if it can get us out of here."

Moving in front of him, she got up on her toes, cupped his cheek, and said, "I don't want you to hurt yourself. There's enough crap up here. Something should be able to help us break through it."

Jilly had never seen Luke worried before, let alone so close to panic. It scared her. She had no idea what she'd do if he succeeded in hurting himself to get them out, because she was not big enough to move him without his help.

"Come on." She tugged on his hand, relieved when he followed her without yanking her arm out of its socket. "Let's sit for a minute and make a plan," she said, grinning. "I like to plan."

His chuckle had the muscles in her shoulders relaxing, but her thighs trembled and need twisted low in her belly. "I remember that about you."

That stopped her in her tracks. "You do?"

Humor, and something else she couldn't define, something darker and hotter that left her breathless, lit in his mismatched eyes. "Are you kidding? I still have the list you made about me when you were in the seventh grade."

Her jaw dropped in sheer embarrassment. Crap, she'd forgotten about that. Trying for her best innocent expression, she blinked. "I don't remember any such list."

"Really?" With a wink, he slipped an all-too-familiar piece of pink paper from his wallet. "Maybe this will jog your memory."

Stunned that he not only still had it, but carried it with him, she collapsed onto the window seat. "You kept it?"

A grin lit his face, something truly wicked dancing in his eyes. "Why would I have gotten rid of it? It's not every day a boy finds a list outlining how his little sister's best friend plans to get him to fall in love with her."

"Oh. My. God." She lowered her head between her legs. "Kill me now."

"Nope." The words were good-natured, and she lifted her head to glare. "Not until you finally appease my curiosity. What exactly does it mean to kiss someone until their head spins?"

"I hate you. You are enjoying this way too much."

He shrugged, still grinning. "Of course I am. Do you blame me?"

"Yes!" Jerking upright, she pointed at him. "It was your own fault. You were always walking around shirtless and sweaty from playing basketball with your friends and whenever you'd see me staring at you, you'd shoot me this wink." Standing, she drilled him in the chest with her finger. "That damned wink kept me obsessed for two years!"

Catching her wrist before she could try to yank free, he hauled her against him, her arm caught between them. All humor faded from his face, replaced with a dark hunger.

"You don't want to talk to me about obsessed, baby. You have no idea what it is to be in love with someone for years and know they're so far out of your reach, you're an idiot for even believing you have a chance. But you can't turn it off. You can't fake your way out of it. All you can do is pray to whatever god feels like listening, that one day you'll wake up and her face won't be the first thing you see. That she won't be the last thing you think about at night, or tonight might finally be the fucking night you stop dreaming of her."

Her mouth dried. "You...me?"

"Yes, goddamn it! You." Gripping her upper arm, he hauled her onto her toes until his mouth hovered directly above hers. "It's always been you."

Without giving her time to process the new information, he swooped in and claimed her mouth again, but that time, he was ravenous. Starving. And with one hand still trapped between them, she had no choice but to meet the storm raging between them head on.

He left her no room for thought. His mouth devoured hers and he dragged her along for the ride.

She was okay with that.

When her legs turned to jelly, he gentled the kiss. If she'd been undone by his raw, possessive hunger, she had no defenses against the tenderness. Slipping a hand over her hip to her bottom, he kept her close while the pad of his other thumb brushed against her cheek.

"Sweet." He licked at her mouth, his tongue sweeping in to alternately destroy and possess as his hand roamed down to palm her breast. With a shuddering groan, he pressed his head against hers. "You are so fucking sweet, baby."

If Jilly had ever had a thought beyond being wrapped naked around Luke Bannon, she could no longer remember it. More importantly, it could be the only thought she had for the rest of her life and she'd be okay with that.

Stepping back, her heart thundering at the devastation on his face, she lifted her shirt over her head. Her jeans came next, until she stood before him in her bra and panties.

Aware it should be a bad idea, she couldn't care less at the moment. Like a switch had been flipped inside of him, he was all over her, his mouth worshipping every inch of skin he found.

"Mine." His hands were gentle as they pulled down the straps of her bra, his lips following the lace-edged material down until his tongue swiped over one nipple. Once. Twice. "Christ, mine."

Sure if he didn't stop she'd go mad, she clasped his head in her hands and arched, desperate for that insanity. She'd never felt so worshipped. Devoured.

Loved.

When his lips closed over her nipple, sucking her into his mouth with a greed that nearly had her coming from the pleasure of it, Jilly was lost.

And so, so screwed.

Chapter Five

So fucking good.

Ignoring the warning klaxons going off in his head, telling him to slow down and think about what the hell he was getting ready to do, Luke hitched her up. He was sure he'd died and gone to heaven when she wrapped her body around him like her life depended on it.

Everything forgotten except the feel of her, the beyond-sweet taste of her, he backed her into the window seat then sat her on it. He fell to his knees in front of her and pulled back, needing to look at her. The fading light from the sun cast a shimmering glow around her, and the words he couldn't say squeezed into his throat, desperate to escape.

He gave up. Tugging her head back, he skimmed his lips up her throat. The erratic pound of her pulse echoed through him, gave him hope where he had no

38

business even wishing for it. But his heart knew she was it for him.

Breath catching on a moan, she clutched his shoulders. Dug in. "Luke. God."

He smiled and continued to trail his mouth over supple skin. Hunger clawed at him while he worshiped her full breasts, tearing moan after moan out of her. And when he dragged his mouth lower, his tongue slicking over her damp panties, her thighs quivered.

His control snapped. With a flick of his fingers, he ripped her panties off and lifted her to his mouth, growling at the taste of her. "So. Fucking. Sweet." Draping her legs over his shoulders, he licked her like a man starved for her taste. Which he was. "Don't move, baby."

Positive she'd keep her legs where he needed them, he relaxed his grip on her thighs and dragged his palm up, until the pad of one thumb scraped against her clit at the same time his tongue dove inside of her. She whimpered, a damp flush covering her, and he grinned.

Then got to work.

Dear God in heaven, he's going to kill me.

She couldn't breathe, couldn't think. Flames licked up her body from the inside out, and if he didn't let her come soon, she'd disintegrate from the pleasure.

"Luke...." He'd lost his hat at some point. Terrified he'd stop and she'd be at the broken edge forever, she tugged at his hair "Please."

Everything in him paused for a heartbeat as his eyes met hers. Pure, dangerous...wickedness dwelled in them. With one final swipe of his tongue, he eased her legs down, then stood.

Shaking too badly to move, she managed to lift her head and nearly drooled while watching him tug off his shirt. A half-gasp, half-moan escaped at her first real glimpse of his massive, muscled torso. Tattoos covered nearly every inch of his flesh, all the way down to ridiculously hot hip muscles.

Next came his pants, followed by black boxer briefs. And when he stood in front of her, gloriously naked, huge, and hard, and...huge, she nearly swallowed her tongue, positive if she didn't get to touch him soon, she'd self-combust.

She started to pull back into a sitting position, but Luke—damn him—had other ideas. In one quick move, he had her in his arms and their positions switched, so she straddled his lap. His cock rubbed against her core, and she moaned, her head falling back in pleasure. His mouth closed over her nipple, worshipping it.

"Christ, baby. I knew you'd feel like heaven." While one hand raked through her hair, the other lowered her down onto his shaft, so slowly she'd have taken over if he hadn't been holding her in an iron grip.

And then—as if sensing how close he'd pushed her to begging—he sucked her breast into his mouth again and drove into her, pushing her over the edge and straight into oblivion.

Her scream triggered a deep growl from him, and, with his gaze locked on hers, he clutched her ass and rocked his hips against hers. Once. Twice. Then he impaled her, so full and thick. A second orgasm built with the force of a freight train. Sure she couldn't stand another second of pleasure, she let her head fell back. He reared up and dragged her mouth to his, all the while driving into her until she worried she'd never again be complete without him.

Left with no choice, she melted into his kiss, gave her body over to him fully, and tumbled one last time into sweet, miraculous oblivion.

And when he buried his face in her throat and

shouted her name, trembling violently, Jilly was a goner.

By the time he'd come down from heaven and was semi-capable of coherent thought, Jilly had collapsed against his chest, boneless and shivering. Sure his world had fallen off its axis, Luke managed to wrap his arms around her and hold on while he waited for the spinning to stop.

Crawling farther up his lap, she curled against him, snuggling in like a cat seeking heat and attention. He smiled and rested his chin on top of her head and ran his fingers through her beautiful hair, grateful for the silence. She'd have questions, and he had no idea how the hell he'd even begin to answer them. Eventually, she shifted against him.

Time's up.

Turning her head, she smiled and pressed a kiss against his chest, directly over his heart, before tilting her head to see his face. "I can honestly say I did not see today ending up this way."

"I'm not going to apologize, Jilly." He straightened, hauling her up with him.

"Luke." Her smile faded a bit, and his heart tumbled to his toes. "I don't want an apology."

42

He closed his eyes. "I know. I'm sorry." Opening his eyes again, he waited for her to meet his gaze. "I didn't expect today to end this way, either. I'm off balance."

She snorted and kissed him on the cheek before climbing off his lap and glancing around for her jeans, giving him the pleasure of watching her bend over to rifle through the pockets. Finding what she'd been looking for, she padded back over and sat beside him then shifted to throw her legs over his and burrow in closer to his side. She shoved a small stack of papers into his hand. "See for yourself."

A smile tugged at his lips. After unfolding the papers, he read the one on top and laughed.

Ways to convince Luke Bannon to keep the house:

1.   Offer to cook for him three times a week. Agree to four if necessary. (Agree to seven days a week.)

2.   Offer to do his laundry.

3.   Offer to make him partner in gift shop/bookstore.

4.   Research ways to out-stubborn stubborn beasts.

5.   Beg.

Guilt mixed with humor, until he kissed the top of

her head, pushed her legs aside, and got to his feet. Handing the rest of the lists back to her, he went to find their clothes. After he'd tugged on his jeans and boots, he rounded up her things.

The vulnerability in her eyes rocked him. With an inward curse for being an asshole, he crouched in front of her and rested his hands on either side of her thighs, crowding her so she had no choice but to look at him.

"I know what this place means to you, baby." He ran his finger up the outside of her thighs. "I know how much you loved your grandmother. But there are some things I can't do, and live here with you is one of them."

Tears welled, but even if she cried, she'd never use it as a weapon against him. Everything affected her so goddamned deep. And he didn't have to hear her say it to understand he had broken her heart.

She sniffed. "I won't bother you."

Christ. He stared at the ceiling, and did his damndest to regain control of his spinning thoughts. While the soft part of him wanted to believe sex could lead to something more, he needed to be rational. There was no guarantee she'd ever love him, and there were some things he couldn't risk.

"It's not about you bothering me. It's about my heart, and how much I can—and can't—take."

Her perfect brow furrowed, confusion flickering in her eyes. But before she could respond, a loud *bang* shattered the room. In the next heartbeat, he shot to his feet, his arms spread to shield Jilly as he tried to figure out what the hell had happened.

The attic door had fallen open.

She crept up against his back, peering around him. "How the hell...?"

Luke shook his head. Grabbing her stuff, he shoved it at her then snagged her hand and dragged her over to the stairs. "Don't question it. Let's just get out of here before it locks us in again." He tossed her clothes down to the hall beneath them before turning toward her then tucked a strand of hair behind her ear. "You go first. I can jump if I need to."

Sky-blue eyes narrowed on him. "You're not going to do something weird and lock yourself up here, are you?"

Unable to block the urge, he brushed a soft kiss over the tip of her nose. Christ, he loved her. "No. I promise."

With a doubtful expression, she nodded. Gaze on his the whole time, she shifted and made her way down the stairs. Back on solid ground again, she scrambled into her clothes, and he followed after her.

Once dressed, he linked their fingers and headed to the first floor. They hadn't solved anything, but he had hope they were no longer locked in this beast of a house. His control and sanity were slipping by the second. If he had to spend one more night with Jilly, he'd end up promising her the moon.

Chapter Six

*W*e're still locked in.

Unease growing in the pit of her stomach, Jilly sat on the stairs while Luke checked every window and door.

When he let out a frustrated sound and sat next to her, she gave a long exhale. "I don't want to bring the mood down or anything, but how worried should we be?"

"I don't know." He rubbed the back of his neck, before bracing his forearms against his knees. "I don't like this. I don't know where it's coming from, and my next option is breaking us out."

Her stomach rolled. "You tried that with the attic door, remember? It didn't work."

He spread his hands, palms up. "What choice do I have?" His hot gaze leveled on hers. "I can't be locked in here with you indefinitely, Jilly."

Any semblance of rational thought vanished as she stared at him. After another moment, he snorted and rose, heading toward the kitchen. Heart aching, she lifted a fist to rub over the traitorous organ. There were a lot of things Jilly wanted in her life. Being something Luke regretted would never be one of them. Her grandmother's will already complicated everything between them. Sex made it even messier.

Not sure what she planned to say to him, but knowing they had to get this figured out, she stood. Any words she'd formed vanished when she walked in. He bent over, his head under the kitchen faucet. *Geez*. The man had an ass that would make most romance cover models jealous.

Fighting the urge to see if a quarter really could bounce off his tight, perfect buns, she cleared her throat and shoved her hands into the back pockets of her jeans. Between his butt and the hint of raw, chiseled torso muscles, thanks to his shirt bunching up, she had to lean against the fridge before she lost her balance.

"Luke?"

His head snapped up, his temple driving straight into the faucet. "Jesus, Jilly," he snapped. Stepping back, he snatched a hand towel from its place on the

48

stove handle and glared at her over his shoulder. "Could you not with that husky voice?"

She winced. "I'm sorry, really. I just...." She'd rather him think her flighty than realize how worried she was that sex with him had opened a floodgate inside of her. Lust, need, wonder, fear, and so many more emotions she couldn't untangle raged through her, all of them—every single goddamned one—directed at, and because of him. "What were you doing?"

A predatory gleam she'd never expected darkened his eyes. He tossed the towel onto the table and stalked toward her.

So busy trying to figure out if she should stand and fight, or flee like the hunted gazelle she felt like, Jilly didn't move, fascinated as he caged her body against the refrigerator, one hand curled around her hip and the other one braced next to her head.

The heat of him threatened to scorch her from the inside out. She tipped her head back and her body arched without her permission until her hardened nipples brushed against the solid wall of his chest.

"What?" He skimmed his nose down her throat. On the way back up, he used his tongue, licking at her skin like she tasted of heaven. "You just...what? Were you watching me, baby?"

Sure her insides had liquefied, Jilly all but melted into a puddle of turned-on female. Despite his smug smirk, or maybe because of it, she wanted to grab his shoulders, haul herself up his body, and plunder his delicious mouth.

She didn't even care her lust for him had come out the blue, slamming into her so hard she'd been blinded by it. And she didn't care it didn't make sense, or that getting sexually involved with him could put her entire future at risk.

Because it was Luke. She'd risk everything for him.

The loud *click,* like pieces of a puzzle she'd never known she should be putting together fell into place, and she jerked.

"Jilly."

Good. God. Low and dark, and somehow wicked, his voice washed over her, tickling her nerve endings until she did a full-body shudder. "Yes?"

His smirk melted into a satisfied, hungry grin. He bent his knees and straightened, bringing her to her toes with him, and settled his hard, muscled thigh right between hers. Sucking in ragged gasps at the intense pressure, if he didn't move his leg soon, he'd feel how much she wanted him when it soaked through both their jeans.

Instead of removing his thigh, he used his grip on her hip to drag her forward, so the friction against her clit had pleasure ripping through her. "It's okay to want me. Christ knows I'm already going crazy needing you again." He skimmed a palm under her shirt and over her belly before cupping her breast, his dark, hypnotic gaze never leaving hers.

The groan of need that escaped him vibrated through her, and she'd never forget the sight of strong, solid Luke closing his eyes, obvious pleasure shuddering through him.

Biting her lip, she lowered the zipper on his jeans and slid her hands behind it, giving in to the urge to squeeze his butt, before she yanked the denim down to his knees.

He caught her when her legs went weak, stormy need in his eyes and...something she couldn't define. Something that came from his very soul. Rising on her toes, she skimmed her lips over his jaw, his mouth, then nipped at his bottom lip before lowering to her knees.

This would be what killed him.

Either that, or he'd already died, gone to heaven,

and Jilly was his reward. Not that he cared which, as long as she didn't stop.

Her tongue worked magic along his cock, licking and teasing, driving him to the brink of insanity over and over again. Then, when his control slipped and he couldn't take any more of the pleasure, needing to be inside her before he came, she swallowed him whole.

He staggered, catching himself on the fridge when his vision grayed and entire world narrowed down to the woman kneeling before him. Grasping the back of her neck, he was torn between wanting to be buried balls-deep between her legs or begging her to never stop the sweet torment of her mouth.

With a monumental orgasm building, he had to pull her away to avoid embarrassment. Helping her to her feet, his heart stuttering at the mix of need and emotion in her eyes, he dragged her shirt over her head, his mouth watering when her breasts bobbed with the motion, her sweet, pretty pink nipples puckered and waiting for his mouth. He licked one, teasing it while he removed her jeans and then, with an almost-savage growl, hitched her up and slammed himself home.

Her head fell back on a scream, a climax rippling

through her and taking him straight to the gates of hell. Working to hold the right angle, he dragged the orgasm out for her. Damp with sweat, he ground his back teeth together with the urge to pound into oblivion inside her.

When her shaking reduced to shivers, he hooked her legs around his waist and fucked them both to madness. He'd never felt anything as perfect as Jilly wrapped around him, clinging, matching him stroke for stroke, giving him everything he demanded of her. He allowed her to keep nothing back as his mouth savaged hers, and his hands possessed.

If she regretted it in the end, he'd deal with that later.

When her body clutched around him again, he swallowed her scream and shoved them both over the edge and into the stars.

***

He had no idea how much time had passed before her small hand pushed against his shoulder. Glancing around the kitchen, he frowned. *What the hell?* "When did we get to the floor?"

"Hmm?" Jilly, sprawled out on her stomach beside

him, lifted her head long enough to push her mass of hair out of her face, her eyes appearing as dazed as he felt. "Unlock the door?"

He chuckled and rose to a sitting position, her sigh of contentment arrowing straight to his heart. Then, with one arm and a quick movement, he had her hauled off the ground and settled in his lap. He'd loved her for five, long goddamned years, before he'd even known what she tasted like. Felt like. How perfectly she responded to him, and fit him. *Now....*

Christ . Now I'm as good as fucked, seven ways to Sunday.

She straightened, nudging his cock with her hip, and a quick grin flashed over her beautiful face when it twitched back to life. Shaking her head, she gripped his face with both hands. "The sink. What were you doing with the sink when I came in?"

"It wasn't working. We don't have electricity either." He frowned when she leapt to her feet. "Jilly?"

When she grabbed her pants, he sat back against the fridge, folding his arms behind his head to watch her struggle into them. He'd have to be dead and buried not to enjoy the sight of her breasts bobbing and swaying with the action, before she bent to grab

54

her shirt.

"I heard a click when we were making out." Pulling her hair out of the back of her shirt, she darted to the sink. Nothing happened when she turned on the faucet, and the lights didn't so much as flicker when she hit the switch. She nibbled on her bottom lip before jogging to the back door. But when that remained locked, she sighed and slumped against the wall. "That was stupid."

Not liking where her thoughts seemed to be taking her, he scowled. "What? It sounds reasonable to me. Last time we had sex, the attic door magically opened. Why wouldn't the back door be unlocked this time?" He snorted at his own words, sure the house, and his non-stop proximity to Jilly, was making him batshit crazy. But he checked the window over the sink anyway.

It opened.

She stood beside him while they gaped at the small opening. Not big enough for even Jilly to fit through, but it was something.

After a long moment, she raised her gaze to his face. "Okay, this may sound crazy, but maybe us having sex really does...unlock things?"

"Yeah. That sounds crazy." But he had no other

explanation. "Stupid question. Has this house ever been haunted?"

Shaking her head, she said, "Not that I know of, but Nana always threated to come back as a ghost and haunt me if I didn't settle down before she died."

He stared at her. "That's crazy."

"I know." Nodding, she added, "But do you have a better explanation?"

"Yes. Kids playing games—"

"And managing to seal every one of the windows and doors, and lock us in the attic?" One brow lifted. "Then unlock the kitchen window—from the inside— without us seeing? While we were screwing each other's brains out?"

His cock leapt to life again, but he forced his brain to focus on the topic at hand. "This house is old, the frames could be warped—"

"Nana said you replaced them all just last year."

Christ. Yeah, he had. Snatching the closest chair, he collapsed into it.

That had been a stupid, insane theory, and he was exhausted. Or Jilly clouded his thinking. But his father had always told him, when all rational theories are exhausted, the only choice left is to accept the fantastical ones.

Luke and Jilly were trapped inside a haunted house.

Chapter Seven

L eave it to her grandmother to haunt her house so Jilly would get a boyfriend.

And not just *a* boyfriend, either. Oh, no, it all made sense now. Nana had never done a single thing in her life without a reason, and Jilly—as well as Luke—had been confused about why the old woman had left him part of her home. Nana didn't want Jilly to end up with just anyone. Nana wanted her with Luke.

The man narrowed his eyes at her. "I'm not going to like whatever you're thinking, am I?"

She offered a shaky smile, doubting he'd love the idea of being part of her grandmother's master plan.

Which brought her to the next question—why had her grandmother chosen him, when Jilly hadn't even told Nana how she felt about him?

"I think it's my Nana," she finally managed. When

his left eye twitched, she wrinkled her nose and wandered to the fridge. Neither of them had eaten in hours. She growled when the door wouldn't even budge. *Seriously?* "Doing the haunting, that is. It's the only thing that makes sense."

He stretched out in his chair and watched her with an intent gaze. Then, crossing his arms, he lifted an eyebrow, all tightly wound, extremely hot, pissed-off male. "How do you figure?"

"How else do you explain inheriting half of my ancestral home? She stuck us together so we'd fall in love."

"Great." His mismatched eyes never left her face, refusing to give her an inch. "She's your grandmother. Tell her she's pissing me—" A drawer across the room flew open with a bang.

A spoon flew at his head, and Jilly yelped and hit the floor. He didn't have time to duck before the projectile grazed his left eye.

"Off," he roared, jumping to his feet, pressing a palm to the injury. "Are you fucking kidding me, you old bat?"

Wise enough to scoot under the kitchen table and cover her head with her arms, Jilly leaned out from under it to glare at him. "Antagonize the ghost, Luke.

59

That'll help. Really." When he growled at her, she shrugged. "No, it's an awesome idea. We have no food, no water, and no way to get out. But let's keep pissing her off."

He half-snorted. "We are not having sex again just to appease your voyeuristic, batshit-crazy grandmother." A plate flew at his head, and that time he did manage to duck before it hit the wall behind him and shattered. Then Luke crouched eye level with her and gave her a pleading look. "Please figure out how to control her."

She gnawed on her bottom lip. "I don't know what she wants. The only thing that makes sense is that she wants us to be...well...together. So she's locking us in."

Temper flickered in the depths of his eyes, one of which had a nasty bruise forming beneath it. He scrubbed a hand over his face and grimaced. "And convincing her it's none of her goddamn business isn't going to work."

"I don't think so." She shook her head and tried to figure out what her grandma's ultimate end goal could be. "How would Nana know that you were attracted to me? We weren't even aware of that fact until two hours ago."

Shifting on a sigh, he sat hard on the floor, and pulled his knees up, bracing his arms against them and watched Jilly. "That's not exactly true."

"How?" She drew her brows together. "I had no clue."

In high school, she'd had a wicked, consuming, teenage-sized crush on him. She'd worshipped the ground he'd walked on and would have given anything for him to notice her. But then she'd met Mike, and her world had fractured at the hands of an abusive, cheating boyfriend. By the time she'd healed and found the missing pieces of herself again, she'd needed the fierce stability Luke—her friend—had offered. And she'd thought she put her foolish, girlish dreams of being with him aside.

"Jesus, Jilly, what more do I have to say to you today to get you to see what's right in front of your face?"

The temper in his words had her head snapping back, and she gaped at him, sure wishful thinking had her imagining the need in his face. Her breath caught somewhere in her lungs as she searched for an answer. "Maybe you should tell me in clear, methodically spelled-out words," she whispered.

"Yeah." Making a frustrated sound, he surged to

his feet. "That's not going to happen. I'll be fucking goddamned before I'm the only vulnerable—Christ!" The freezer door popped open and bashed him in the back of the head. He hit the floor. "Fine! You win, you crazy old woman!" Rising to his knees, he glared at Jilly, more pissed off and...vulnerable than she'd ever thought possible. "I love you. All right?" He shifted his gaze to the ceiling. "Are you fucking happy now?"

In answer, the faucet emitted one loud gurgle before water gushed in a steady stream.

Luke stared at the faucet, the ceiling, the floor. Anywhere but at Jilly. He didn't need to see the doubt and regret flickering over her beautiful face, his heart in his goddamned throat while waiting to see which emotion she finally settled on. The woman owned his heart, and it exhausted him. Exhausted him to know he'd never have her, that she was just out of reach. His choices with her were to either break her heart and force her to give up her family's home, or live in misery for the rest of his life.

They weren't options. They were Fate's way of laughing at him.

"Wait. You love me?"

"No." He shook his head, and stared at a blank

space on the wall, not caring if it made him a chickenshit. Anything was better than being honest. "That would make me the biggest, most masochistic asshole on the face of the Earth."

"Luke." She scooted a little closer to him. "You love me."

"Just...hell, Jilly. Drop it. For the love of fucking Christ, pretend I didn't say that."

"I can't." Cupping his face, she forced him to look at her. "I don't want to."

Damn it all, he hated feeling vulnerable. She held his whole damned world in her tiny hands while he risked everything. It didn't sit well with him. "Why not?"

She rubbed her fist over her chest. "I've made a lot of mistakes. I've made bad choices and screwed up. But somewhere in the back of my mind, deep in the darkest, most sheltered part of my heart, I've always been in love with you. So I got really good at pretending we were just friends."

Too pissed off and edgy to give her grandmother any more of a show, he didn't mean to move, but if Jilly was playing with him...he gripped her hips.

"Mean it." The words grated out in a voice more animalistic than his own. "I swear to God, don't play

63

with me."

Resting her head against his shoulder, she shifted closer. "I'm not. I wouldn't." The sudden uncertainty in her face killed him. "I guess Nana remembered how I used to babble about you in high school and assumed that I'd never gotten over you. I didn't even realize it until being locked in here with you today."

He hooked an arm around her waist and hauled her into his lap. "Say it again."

Her teeth bit into her bottom lip and she graced him with a crooked grin. "Okay. You love me. You, Luke Bannon, love me."

Relief and emotion flashed through him, until he was grateful he wasn't on his feet. No way would his legs hold them both right then, and he couldn't imagine setting her down. He nodded and kissed her once, with all the love and tenderness in his heart. "I love you. Now put me out of my misery and tell me you love me."

"It's funny." Light dancing in her eyes, she grinned up at the ceiling. "I never would have thought—"

He gave a warning growl. "Jilly, I mean—"

"Hush, now." She patted his chest then let out a whooping laugh when he tucked her body under his and sprawled her out on the kitchen floor. His heart, already hers for so damned long, took a slow tumble at the emotion dancing in her laughing sky-blue eyes. "I love you. Happy now?"

He kissed her, his laugh coming from his very soul. "Delirious."

As she kissed him back, a distinct *click* echoed.

They were free.

Epilogue

Jilly sat cross-legged in the middle of the living room floor, with notes and lists— color-coded—fanned out around her, and winced after glancing at her watch. Luke would be back with the lawyers in less than twenty minutes, and she hadn't solidified her argument yet.

The last week had flown by in a blur of happiness and lust and so much sex, it honestly surprised her she still managed to walk. Not that she'd ever complain. Sex with Luke would never, ever be a hardship and honestly, even after the last week of spending time exclusively with him, it still thrilled her the way he couldn't walk past her without touching her. The way he brushed his fingertips against the ends of her hair when they sat together. Or the way she'd wake up every morning to his legs tangled around hers, her head tucked up against his chest like he'd reached for her in his sleep and couldn't let her go. She loved it all. Every second of it.

And she *loved* him. Not that she ever forgot, but it reminded her of the grief she still felt for her Nana—it hadn't gone away, her brain accepted it, but every once in a while, it would come out of nowhere and blindside her, knocking her on her butt no matter where she happened to be. Jilly would look at him and all the love and grief inside of her would wrap around her heart and squeeze until breathing through it almost hurt.

But while they'd spent nearly every second of every day together, they'd avoided the one subject they most needed to discuss—what to do with St. James Manor.

It had been a touchy subject before they'd realized her Nana had turned into a ghost to get her way, but, more than anything, Jilly didn't want Luke to think she'd use him to get what she wanted.

The funny thing—while spending hours methodically listing her arguments and color-coding them according to strength of that particular argument, she understood, yeah, St. James Manor meant a lot to her. But Luke was her home now. Whether they settled in her family's ancestral home or a shack in the backwoods of some forgotten forest, she'd make it work, as long as she had him.

In only a week, he'd become the one thing she couldn't bear to lose.

The back door opened, followed by three pairs of footsteps, and she braced for the news.

"Jilly, baby? Are you…. Crap." Luke crouched in front of her, mismatched eyes shadowed beneath his ratty ball cap. "What's up, babe? Are you planning on invading Russia?"

Snorting out a laugh, she accepted his help getting to her feet. "That would probably be easier." Drawing in a deep breath, she ignored the two lawyers crowding the doorway behind her. "We haven't discussed the house since Nana unlocked us, and our time is up."

Surprise flicked in his gorgeous eyes. His gaze dropped to her meticulously organized notes then back to her face. "That's because my mind has been made up since then." He lifted a brow and crossed his arms. "But feel free to argue your points. I don't want you to have wasted all this time."

She waved that off. "It's never a waste, trust me. But, Luke…." She stepped over her rainbow of notes with care until she stood directly in front of him.

After all her planning and plotting, none of it really mattered. "I don't care where we live. I don't want to be somewhere that makes you miserable, and you said yourself, updating this place would be a decade out of your life. I just want to be with you." She lifted her chin in defiance of how cheesy the next sentence would sound. "You're my home."

A full ten seconds passed before he let out a sigh. "That's it? That's your argument?" With a disappointed expression, he shook his head. "I expected a full-on PowerPoint presentation, including charts and graphs, and hours and hours of arguments."

Her heart knocked against her chest because for the first time all week, she couldn't tell if he was teasing or serious. "I have all of that," she said, heat blooming on her face, "but I don't want you to do this because I wore you down."

The quick shrug had her heart leaping into her throat. When had her Luke turned cold? "It doesn't matter." He gestured at the lawyers still standing behind her. "The paperwork has already been filled out. It just needs your signature."

She blinked, but quick on the heels of the hurt came anger, and she shouted, "You...you.... You made a decision without me?"

Confusion flickered over his face before he waved the men forward. "I didn't think you'd care, baby. All you have to do is sign, and this place is ours forever."

"Of course I care—what?" She could only stare as the taller of the two old men started unloading files from his briefcase. "What's going on?"

"I love you, Jilly."

Nodding, she acknowledged his words, but her gaze never left the attorney, sure she'd missed something. "That's nice, and you know I love you, too, but—"

"Baby. I need you to look at me."

She did, and her heart finally caught up with what her brain tried to tell her. Kneeling on one knee, he held a small black box in his hands. He'd removed the ball cap while she gaped at him, and his heart, so full of love for her, was in his beautiful, mismatched eyes.

Twining the fingers of his free hand around hers, he said, "I love you. I couldn't live in this place with you while knowing I could never have you. It would have killed me to see you dating other men, knowing they had the right to touch you, kiss you, be with you, when I knew it should have been me. I wouldn't have survived it. But then your pain-in-the-ass Nana locked us in here, and you knocked down every wall I'd built to keep my heart intact. And I realized, no matter how much I'd loved you before, it was nothing compared to what I felt after being able to touch you the way I'd desperately needed to for all these years."

He closed his eyes and cleared the emotion out of his throat before he looked at her again and traced his thumb over the trail of tears leaking down her face. "I'm asking you to marry me. It doesn't have to be now, or even in a year. But this house is ours, and I want us to live here in it, together, as a couple. Not mine and yours, but ours. And I need you to know that this isn't temporary for me. It's forever. So say yes to me, Jilly. Say you'll be with me until we both die of old age and can come back and haunt our grandchildren together."

She opened her mouth to answer him, but nothing she could say felt like enough. Swiping at her tears and sniffling pathetically, she fell to her knees and let him see the love and desperate need inside her. Wrapping herself around him, she rested her head against his. The words she finally gave him were the only ones that mattered because her heart had long ago made the decision for her.

So, with all the joy and love she had, she nodded

while her entire world narrowed to him. Always him.

"Forever, Luke. You're all I need."

About the Author

Convinced dragons have gotten a bad rep throughout time, and more than a little addicted to fairy tales and romance novels, Eden Ashe has decided to re-write history. In her version, the dragons are ancient warriors in tarnished armor, who not only deserve the girl in the end, but will fight forever for her.